This book belongs to

....

....

....

Colleen Dixon

COCO LOVES HER CURLY HAIR

Coco loves when her mummy
Styles her curly hair.
She wakes up eager every morning
And sits in her purple chair.

Coco can't wait to plan
Her every style and tweak.
She thinks about her style for Monday
And all through the week.

On Monday, Coco was ready for her first style.
"I want big blue bobbles in my hair!"
She said with a smile.

Coco watched her mummy
Tie blue bobbles in her hair.

"Wow!" Coco said,
"They match the blue dress I'm going to wear."

The following day was Tuesday,
And Coco couldn't wait.
Her next hairstyle
Was going to be great!

"Today, I want a bow in my hair.
And two big puffs, larger than a bear!"

Coco's mummy tied her hair
In two large puffs on her head.

She loved them so much,
She even wore them to bed!

Wednesday came around
And Coco had a new plan for her hair.
"I want ten beautiful twists!" Coco said.
"Everywhere all over my head!"

Coco's mummy brushed,
Twisted and twirled.
"There you go, Coco;
You are the most beautiful
Girl in the world!"

Thursday was next, and you won't believe
What Coco had planned.
She asked her mummy for Bantu knots,
Which were very large and grand.

"Wow!"

It was Friday!
Coco's favourite day of the week.
She climbed into her chair
And waited for her mummy
To cornrow her hair.

Saturday morning came,
And Coco had a secret to share:
She wanted colourful bands all over her hair.
"I want more colours than any rainbow
you've ever seen!"

Coco's mummy gave her a mirror
And watched her face gleam.

Sunday came, and Coco had a lot to say
About the style she had planned for that day!
"Mummy, I want bouncy braids in my hair.
Braids, braids everywhere!"

Coco was so happy with her braids,
She even did a twirl!

"Thank you, Mummy.
You're the best mum in the whole world!"

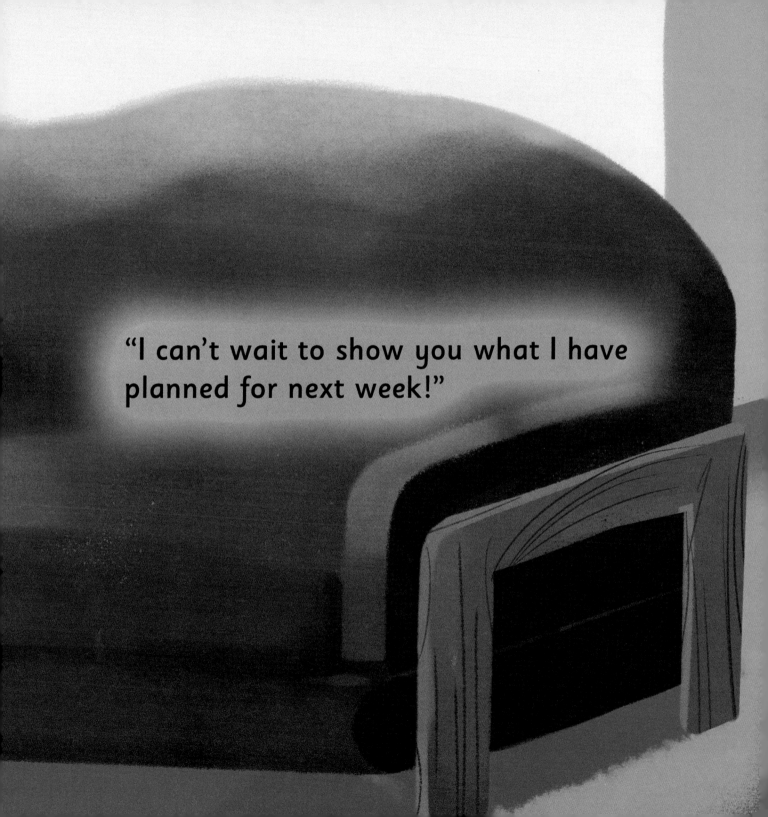

Made in the USA
Monee, IL
26 September 2020